This edition published in 1993 by Mimosa Books,
distributed by Outlet Book Company, Inc., a Random House Company,
40 Engelhard Avenue, Avenel, New Jersey 07001.

2 4 6 8 10 9 7 5 3 1

First published in 1993 by Grisewood & Dempsey Ltd.
Copyright © Grisewood & Dempsey Ltd.1984, 1991, 1993

ISBN 1 85698 500 8

Printed and bound in Italy

LITTLE BO PEEP

AND OTHER NURSERY RHYMES

MIMOSA
·BOOKS·

NEW YORK • AVENEL, NEW JERSEY

ONE, TWO

1, 2,
Buckle my shoe;

3, 4,
Knock at the door;

5, 6,
Pick up sticks;

7, 8,
Lay them straight;

9, 10,
A big fat hen;

11, 12
Dig and delve;

13, 14,
Maids a-courting;

15, 16,
Maids in the kitchen;

17, 18,
Maids a-waiting;

19, 20,
My plate's empty.

LAVENDER'S BLUE

Lavender's blue, dilly, dilly,
    Lavender's green,
When I am king, dilly, dilly,
    You shall be queen.

Call up your men, dilly, dilly,
    Set them to work,
Some to the plow, dilly, dilly,
    Some to the cart.

Some to make hay, dilly, dilly,
    Some to thresh corn,
Whilst you and I, dilly, dilly,
    Keep ourselves warm.

TO THE SNAIL

Snail, snail, put out your horns,
And I'll give you bread and barley corns.

HODDLEY, PODDLEY

Hoddley, poddley, puddle and fogs,
Cats are to marry the poodle dogs;
Cats in blue jackets and dogs in red hats,
What will become of the mice and the rats?

HANNAH BANTRY

Hannah Bantry,
In the pantry,
Gnawing at a mutton bone;
How she gnawed it,
How she clawed it,
When she found herself alone.

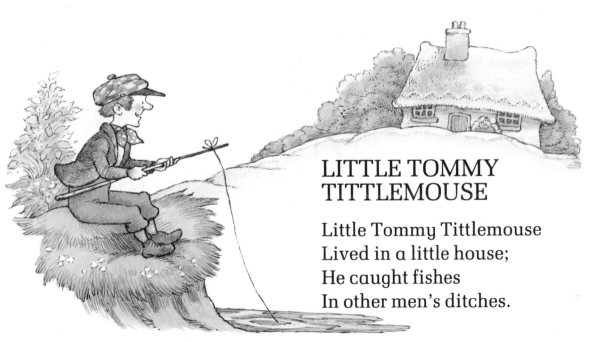

LITTLE TOMMY TITTLEMOUSE

Little Tommy Tittlemouse
Lived in a little house;
He caught fishes
In other men's ditches.

THE MISCHIEVOUS RAVEN

A farmer went trotting upon his gray mare,
    Bumpety, bumpety, bump!
With his daughter behind him so rosy and fair,
    Lumpety, lumpety, lump!

A raven cried, Croak! and they all tumbled down,
    Bumpety, bumpety, bump!
The mare broke her knees and the farmer his crown,
    Lumpety, lumpety, lump!

The mischievous raven flew laughing away,
    Bumpety, bumpety, bump!
And vowed he would serve them the same the next day,
    Lumpety, lumpety, lump!

ON SATURDAY NIGHT

On Saturday night I lost my wife,
And where do you think I found her?
Up in the moon, singing a tune,
And all the stars around her.

POLLY

Polly, put the kettle on,
Polly, put the kettle on,
Polly, put the kettle on,
   We'll all have tea.

Sukey, take it off again,
Sukey, take it off again,
Sukey, take it off again,
   They've all gone away.

TO THE RAIN

Rain, rain, go away,
Come again another day,
Little Johnny wants to play.
Rain, rain, go to Spain,
Never show your face again.

STAR LIGHT

Star light, star bright,
First star I see tonight,
I wish I may, I wish I might,
Have the wish I wish tonight.

YANKEE DOODLE

Yankee Doodle came to town,
    Riding on a pony,
He stuck a feather in his cap
    And called it macaroni.

ROSES ARE RED

Roses are red,
Violets are blue,
Sugar is sweet
And so are you.

EENTSY WEENTSY

Eensty Weensty spider
    Went up the garden spout;
Down came the rain
    And washed the spider out;
Out came the sun
    And dried up all the rain;
Eentsy Weentsy spider,
    Went up the spout again.

TO THE LADYBUG

Ladybug, Ladybug,
  Fly away home,
Your house is on fire
  Your children all gone;
All but one,
  And her name is Ann,
And she has crept under
  The warming pan.

JEREMIAH

Jeremiah, blow the fire,
  Puff, puff, puff!
First you blow it gently,
  Then you blow it rough.

LITTLE BO-PEEP

Little Bo-peep has lost her sheep,
   And can't tell where to find them;
Leave them alone, and they'll come home,
   Bringing their tails behind them.

Little Bo-peep fell fast asleep,
   And dreamed she heard them bleating;
But when she awoke, she found it a joke,
   For they were still a-fleeting.

Then up she took her little crook,
    Determined for to find them;
She found them indeed, but it made her heart bleed
    For they'd left their tails behind them.

It happened one day, as Bo-peep did stray
    Into a meadow hard by,
There she espied their tails side by side,
    All hung on a tree to dry.

She heaved a sigh, and wiped her eye,
    And over the hillocks went rambling,
And tried what she could as a shepherdess should,
    To tack each again to its lambkin.

BOBBY SHAFTOE

Bobby Shaftoe's gone to sea,
Silver buckles on his knee;
He'll come back and marry me,
    Bonny Bobby Shaftoe.

Bobby Shaftoe's bright and fair,
Combing down his yellow hair,
He's my love for evermore,
    Bonny Bobby Shaftoe.

RIDE A COCK-HORSE

Ride a cock-horse to Banbury Cross,
To see a fine lady upon a white horse;
Rings on her fingers and bells on her toes,
She shall have music wherever she goes.

THE BELLS OF LONDON

Oranges and lemons,
Say the bells of St. Clement's.

You owe me five farthings,
Say the bells of St. Martin's.

When will you pay me?
Say the bells of Old Bailey.

When I grow rich,
Say the bells of Shoreditch.

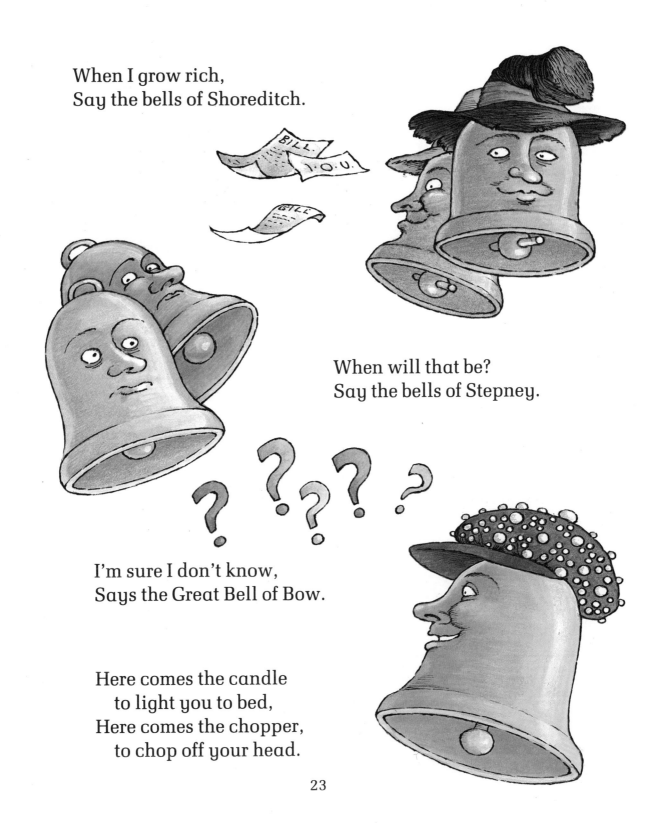

When will that be?
Say the bells of Stepney.

I'm sure I don't know,
Says the Great Bell of Bow.

Here comes the candle
    to light you to bed,
Here comes the chopper,
    to chop off your head.

TWINKLE, TWINKLE

Twinkle, twinkle, little star,
How I wonder what you are!
Up above the world so high,
Like a diamond in the sky.

JACK HORNER

Little Jack Horner
Sat in the corner,
Eating his Christmas pie;
He put in his thumb,
And pulled out a plum,
And said, What a good boy am I!

POP GOES THE WEASEL!

Up and down the City Road,
   In and out the Eagle,
That's the way the money goes,
   Pop goes the weasel!

Half a pound of tuppeny rice,
   Half a pound of treacle,
Mix it up and make it nice,
   Pop goes the weasel!

Every night when I go out
   The monkey's on the table;
Take a stick and knock it off,
   Pop goes the weasel!